THE SMALLEST CHRISTMAS

Written and illustrated by
LINDA CARDILLO

Bellastoria Press
Longmeadow, Massachusetts

Bellastoria Press
P.O. Box 60341
Longmeadow, Massachusetts 01116

Cover design by
Dar Albert, Wicked Smart Designs

For Stephan, Luke, Nicola and Mark

"No Christmas tree this year,"

said Papa as the family lit the first candle on their Advent wreath.

The wreath sat in the middle of their dining table, which was the only thing in the living room of their new house except for the piano.

It was their first night in the new house. The room didn't even have any lights yet, just the shimmering firelight of the Advent candle.

It was Maria who first reacted to Papa's announcement.

"Oh, no! We have to have a Christmas tree! We always have a Christmas tree!" She had her hands on her hips and sounded quite indignant. Sometimes she had a very large voice for such a small person. She had just turned four.

"I was really looking forward to having a tree," added her ten-year-old brother, Jack. He was trying very hard not to let his disappointment show.

"Why can't we have a tree?" Maria wanted to know.

"Because we won't be here to enjoy the tree or take care of it. With no one here to water the tree it would dry out. We would arrive home to a big pile of brown needles on the floor."

"We'll have other trees at Oma's house in Connecticut and Nanna and Poppa's house in Florida," Papa added, reminding the children that they would be visiting their German grandmother, Oma, and their Italian grandparents, Nanna and Poppa, during the holidays.

"Yes, but none of them will be *our* tree," protested Jack. "In my *whole* life we've always had a Christmas tree at home even when we visited our grandparents. This will be the first time ever that we don't have our own tree."

"Before now, we only went away for a few days. This time, because we live so far away from our family, we have a long way to travel to visit them. We'll be gone almost a whole month. That is just too long to leave a tree in the house."

Papa's voice had that sound to it that meant the discussion was over.

The children were sad and disappointed. The house was going to feel empty indeed without a Christmas tree.

Maria and Jack's family had just moved into their new house in a small village on the Rhine River in Germany. They had arrived in Germany three months before and had been living in a hotel until Mama found the house. Everyone was happy that they finally had a home.

 They had come from America, where they had lived in a tall wooden house that stood high on a ridge in the middle of woods filled with old oak trees. From the highest windows in the house in the wintertime you could see the hills all around. And on crystal clear days, if you stood on the flat roof, it had been said that you could see the ocean fifty miles away (although they had never seen it themselves).

Maria and Jack missed their old home. They especially missed the animals who lived on the ridge with them—the deer, the raccoons, the woodchucks, the squirrels and chipmunks, and the hawks.

Their new home in Germany was a stone house attached to two other houses on a street with lots of neighbors close by. The children hadn't seen any animals yet except for Bobby, their next-door neighbor's extremely small dog.

The family had come to live in Germany for a few years while Papa worked there. He had been born in Germany and had lived there as a little boy. Now that he was grown up and had children of his own, he was excited that his family would come to know the land of his birth. Over the next few days the family worked together at getting settled. In the mornings everyone went to school. Maria went to kindergarten in Eltville. Jack went to St. Ursula's School in Geisenheim. Mama and Papa went to language school in Wiesbaden.

In the afternoons Papa went to work and Mama, Maria and Jack unpacked boxes.

One afternoon, Mama and the children were opening cartons in the basement, unwrapping dishes and pots and stacking them carefully on the floor. Maria got distracted and started playing with the wooden spoons and containers as she unpacked them. One of her favorite games was playing "kitchen." It was then that Jack discovered the two Christmas boxes.

"Look what I found!" he called out.

He waded carefully across the room through the huge piles of wrapping paper and dishes stacked on the floor. He had two cardboard boxes, one large and one small, balanced precariously in his arms. On the outside of the large box, in big black letters, it said "XMAS." The small box was marked "MANGER."

"Can we open them, please, Mom, please?"

Mama had her head down inside one of the dish cartons, retrieving the turkey platter. When she emerged, her hair was falling out of the knot she wore on top of her head and her chin was smudged. She looked around—at the piles of paper and dishes, at the stacks of boxes that still hadn't been opened—and didn't see the letters on the boxes Jack was carrying. What she saw instead was "MESS."

"Absolutely not," she said. "I don't know where I'm going to put half of the stuff we *need*," she told Jack. "I can't even begin to think about where to put the stuff we don't need. And right now, because we aren't going to put up a tree this year, we certainly don't need Christmas decorations. Now put those boxes back in the corner out of the way and help me make some room here."

Mama was frazzled.

Jack decided to try one more time. "Couldn't we at least take out the manger? We don't need a tree to set up the manger, do we?"

Mama was about to say no again.

That it was too much work.

That they had other more important things to do to get settled.

But then she stopped herself.

She was remembering when she first bought the manger. Jack was three and attending a day care center at the university where Papa was studying. The children who went to the center came from all over the world. In December the parents took turns visiting the center to tell the children how they celebrated the season in their own countries.

Mama decided to tell the children the Christmas story of Jesus' birth and how people remembered the birth by setting up a manger, with statues of donkeys and cows and shepherds and Jesus, Mary and Joseph.

She went to a shop near St. Patrick's Cathedral in New York City and bought a manger with statues that wouldn't break so the children could touch them. After that it became her children's special Christmas job to set up the manger.

"OK," she nodded.

She put down the turkey platter, dusted off her hands and led the way up to the living room, closing the door to the basement and the mess.

Jack and Maria wiped the dust from the stable and put it on top of the piano. Then they carefully unwrapped each figure, which had been packed the year before in white tissue paper with blue stars.

Soon, almost everyone was in the stable—Mary and Joseph, the cow and the donkey, and the shepherds and their sheep.

And then, at last, they gently placed the Baby Jesus in the manger.

Mama smiled.

She was glad that she had "yes" to the manger.

As soon as Papa came home that evening, the children rushed him into the living room to see the manger. He smiled too.

After dinner, with the Advent candles lit in the middle of the table (now there were three), the family worked on their Christmas cards. Instead of buying cards they always made their own, with everyone helping.

That Christmas Jack folded origami stars out of colored paper; Maria and Papa glued them onto the cards; and Mama wrote the greeting inside.

In just a few more days they would be flying back to America to celebrate Christmas. There was still so much to do. Mama and Papa hadn't finished their Christmas shopping yet and Jack was still making Christmas tree ornaments to give as presents.

Everyone was busy, tired and a little bit cranky.

The next day was grey and rainy. By the evening a gusty wind was blowing down from the hills above the village. Papa was on his way home from work, walking briskly through the rain and wind from the train station. It was a lonely evening. There was no one else out on the street and most people had already closed their rolling shutters and were snug inside their houses.

Suddenly Papa noticed something unusual in the quiet, deserted street. It tumbled and skittered toward him, carried swiftly by the wind. When it reached Papa's feet it stopped, as if it had reached its destination.

It was the smallest Christmas tree he had ever seen!

It was about two feet tall and gently tapered from the tip to the wider branches at the bottom.

Papa looked around, wondering if someone had been chasing after the tree as it escaped in the wind, but there was still no one else in the street. He shrugged and shook his head. He bent down and picked it up.

"I guess you were meant for me, little one. Well, come on then, let's go home."

He tucked the tree under his arm and walked up the street.

He let himself quietly into the house. Everyone was in the kitchen getting ready for dinner. Maria burst through the door, dancing. "Papa's home! Papa's home!" And then, "What's that? What did you bring? Jack, Mama, come and see!"

The whole family crowded into the hall to see Papa's surprise.

"This found me on the way home tonight. I think we were meant to have a tree this year after all," he explained, smiling as he held up the little tree, still dripping and glistening from the rain.

Jack and Maria were so happy and excited that they couldn't keep still. They both were jumping up and down, shouting.

"Hurray! Hurray! We have a Christmas tree!"

Mama shook her head in wonderment.

"Where? How?" she asked Papa.

He described to everyone how the little tree had flown down the street and landed at his feet.

"It looks like it might be a piece of a much larger tree. Maybe someone in the neighborhood bought a tree that was too big and had to cut it," she suggested. But the children didn't seem to hear. They didn't need explanations. They weren't puzzled, because they knew.

The little tree was a special, magical gift.

Somehow, the tree had reached them. Maybe it was an angel's breath itself that had blown the tree down the road to Papa.

Jack and Maria were already planning the decorations. "...and we've got to make some popcorn to string into a garland, and then..."

"Whoa," said Mama. "We're leaving on the day after tomorrow and there's still a lot to be done to get ready. We don't have time to spend hours decorating a tree."

Mama, again, was thinking about the mess, and the laundry, and the packing and....

Everyone turned to look at her in disbelief.

She saw three eager faces—Jack, Maria and Papa—filled with the delight of Papa's discovery. Sometimes when she was busy and had too much to do, Mama forgot what was important to children. But she was lucky, because she had three reminders ready to bring her back to those important things.

"OK, OK," she grinned. "Right after supper."

That evening, Papa went down to the cellar and carried up the big carton with the "XMAS" label that Jack had found earlier in the week. Inside were smaller boxes filled with the ornaments the family had collected or made over many years.

There were too many for such a small tree, so they picked out their favorites:

A wooden bird painted bright red

A blue bell that had hung on Mama's family tree

when she was a little girl

and a straw star that had been a gift from Oma.

The tip of the tree was too weak to hold the star they usually hung on the top of their Christmas trees. In its place Mama pinned a tiny painted angel to a red ribbon and tied the ribbon to a gold bow at the top of the tree.

The trunk of the little tree was too narrow for their Christmas tree stand, but Papa was able to get it to work with some pieces of wood. He also hooked up a string of white lights.

At the bottom of the tree Mama spread a bright red tablecloth.

When they were finished and every carefully chosen ornament was in exactly the right place, Papa plugged in the lights.

"It's the smallest Christmas tree we've ever had,"

someone whispered. "But it's the best."

 Linda Cardillo survived three months in a hotel room in a foreign country with two kids, a hot plate and one pot before her family moved into a house in a small German village just before Christmas. She emerged from the packing boxes not only to find her turkey platter but also to write this story for her children.

Please visit her website at www.lindacardillo.com or write her at linda@lindacardillo.com

27695485R00024

Made in the USA
Lexington, KY
19 November 2013